Ann's Extraordinary Experiment

"Coloured Bedtime StoryBook"

By

Nandita Jayaraj

Illustrated by

Priya Kuriyan

ILLUSTRATED & PUBLISHED
BY
E-KİTAP PROJESİ & CHEAPEST BOOKS

www.cheapestboooks.com

 www.facebook.com/EKitapProjesi

ISBN: 978-625-6308-89-3

Copyright, 2024 by e-Kitap Projesi
Istanbul

Categories: Science, Problem Solving & Critical Thinking
Country of Origin: United States
Cover: © Cheapest Books
License: CC-BY-4.0

For full terms of use and attribution, http://creativecommons.org/licenses/by/4.0/

Contributing: Priya Kuriyan

© **All rights reserved**.

Except for the conditions stated in the License, no part of this book shall be reproduced or transmitted in any form or by any means, electronic or mechanical, including photocopy, recording or by any information or retrieval system, without written permission form the publisher.

About the Book

Anna Mani was an Indian scientist who loved to read about the world around her. Peek into her eighth birthday party and follow her through her extraordinary scientific adventures.

Ann's Extraordinary Experiment

Nandita Jayaraj
Priya Kuriyan

"Foooo! Foooo!" Anna Mani blew out all eight candles on her birthday cake.

"Happy Birthday, Anna!" shouted her brothers and sisters.

Anna had a big family and a big house on a hill. But on her birthday, she had only one small wish.

Anna tore open her birthday gift and peered in.

There was something sparkling inside.

"Diamond earrings? Aiyye!" She did not want diamond earrings.

They were expensive and useless!

Do you know what Anna really wished for?

Books, books and more books!

"We have books at home!" said her brother. But Anna had already read those.

"There are more in the library!" pointed out her grandfather. But Anna had read those too!

She marched into her room. "Hmmph!"

Later that day, there was a knock on Anna's door. But there was nobody outside!
Instead, there lay a big box at her doorstep.
"This better not be more jewellery!" she said loudly. It wasn't. It was a brand new set of Encyclopaedia books!
"So many books. Hurray!" Anna ran around her house, hugging everyone.

Many years later, and many, many, many books later, Anna found a job in the laboratory of a famous scientist.

"What should I do here?" asked Anna. The scientist pointed to a box.

What do you think she found inside?

"Diamonds? Aiyyyye!" said Anna.

But this time, the diamonds were not to be worn. They were for experiments.

The scientist wanted Anna to find out what makes diamonds shine. So she read books about diamonds.

Books, books and more books!

Being a scientist was the best! She could study anything she wanted.

Anna did like things that shine. And what shines brighter than diamonds?

The sun!

So Anna read books about the sun, sunlight and the weather.

Books, books and more books!

Anna did hundreds of experiments.
She built many gadgets that could measure the weather of a place.

How sunny is it in Bombay?

Anna built a gadget to measure that.

How windy is it in Madras?

Anna built a gadget for that too.

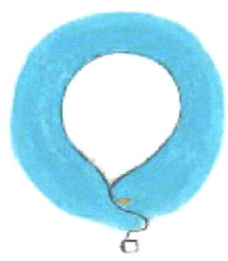

Her favourite gadget took many months to build.

It is a special balloon called an ozonesonde. It has a small machine fixed to it. The machine can measure a gas found in air called ozone.

It can fly really high.

Look, there goes Anna's ozonesonde!

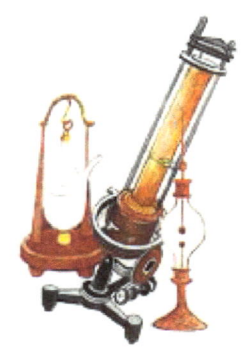

Guess how many gadgets Anna Mani built in all?

Nearly one hundred weather gadgets!

She even had her own factory where these were made. It was as if she could build anything!

Anna Mani became one of the wisest weather scientists in India.

Even as she grew older and more well known, her best friends remained the same.

Books, books and more books!

Life & Times of Anna: A Timeline

23 August, 19 18 - Anna Mani is born in Peermedu in Kerala.

19 40 - She gets a scholarship to work at CV Raman's laboratory in Bangalore.

19 45 - She leaves for England to study Meteorology.

19 48 - She returns and joins the Indian Meteorological Department in Pune.

19 62 - She starts work on the ozonesonde project.

19 76 - She retires as Deputy Director General of the Indian Meteorological department.

In the 19 80 s(exact year unknown) - She starts her own company to manufacture her gadgets.

16 August, 20 01 - Anna Mani passes away in Kerala.

Wonderful Weather Words

Meteorologist (say it like this: 'meet-your-all-o-jist'):

A meteorologist is a scientist who studies the weather and climate of a region. Anna Mani was one of the best meteorologists there ever was!

Ozonesonde (say it like this: 'oh-zone-sond'): Ozonesondes are balloons which fly high up into the sky. The balloons have gadgets fixed to them which measure the amount of ozone present in the air. Ozone is important because it blocks out harmful light coming from the sun. Too little ozone high up in in the sky means we are in trouble!

If you could be a scientist, what would you want to study?

A Note on the Book

This story is a work of creative non-fiction based on the life of Anna Mani.

End of the Story

www.ingramcontent.com/pod-product-compliance
Lightning Source LLC
LaVergne TN
LVHW070453080526
838202LV00035B/2822